The Penny Tree

Text copyright © 1994 by Willard Reese

First printed in 1994 5 4 3 2 1

Canadian Cataloguing in Publication Data

Reese, Will, 1925-
  The penny tree

    First ed. has title: The money tree.
    ISBN 1-55105-050-1

    I. Switzer, Phil. II. Title. III. Title: The money tree.
PS8585.E44P4 1994   jC813'.54   C94-910814-6
PZ7.R43Pe 1994

Illustrations copyright © 1994 by Philip Switzer

Printed in Canada

The Publisher: Lone Pine Publishing
206, 10426–81 Avenue, Edmonton, Alberta, Canada T6E 1X5
202A, 1110 Seymour Street, Vancouver, B.C., Canada V6B 3N3
16149 Redmond Way, #180, Redmond, Washington, USA 98052

The publisher gratefully acknowledges the assistance of Alberta Community Development and the Department of Canadian Heritage, the support of the Canada/Alberta Agreement on the cultural industries, and the financial support provided by the Alberta Foundation for the Arts.

The Penny Tree

Written by Will Reese
Illustrated by Phil Switzer

LONE PINE

"What's that?" asked Jen,
        "Here! Under this rock!"

We were both out exploring
        around our block.

"It looks like a map
        of the neighbourhood.

"It says 'TREASURE MAP.'
        This could be good!"

The squiggly letters
were hard to read,

But we figured them out
to see where they'd lead:

"*This ancient chart
marks a secret treasure,*

"*So follow each turn
and check every measure.*"

We carefully studied
     the mysterious chart.

It said that the rock
     was the place to start.

"Read on!" Jen pleaded.
     "Quick, tell me more!

"What is this treasure
     we're hunting for?"

The map explained the mystery:

It said the **X** marked a Penny Tree,

Where pennies fell each Friday night,

And sparkled in the morning light.

We followed the map,
    we raced and we flew,

'Til we reached the yard
    of a house we knew...

"Yikes! That must be the tree!"
    I said, disgusted,

"If we trespass in there
    we're going to get busted!"

"You're right!" cried Jen. "Let's check it again.

"Old Man Bowers is nobody's friend."

So we followed the map more carefully,

But we still came back to the same darn tree.

Bowers lived all alone.
    He was mean. He was hard.

No kids ever played
    in that old man's yard.

We were scared to sneak in,
    but we had to see

If there really were pennies
    under that tree.

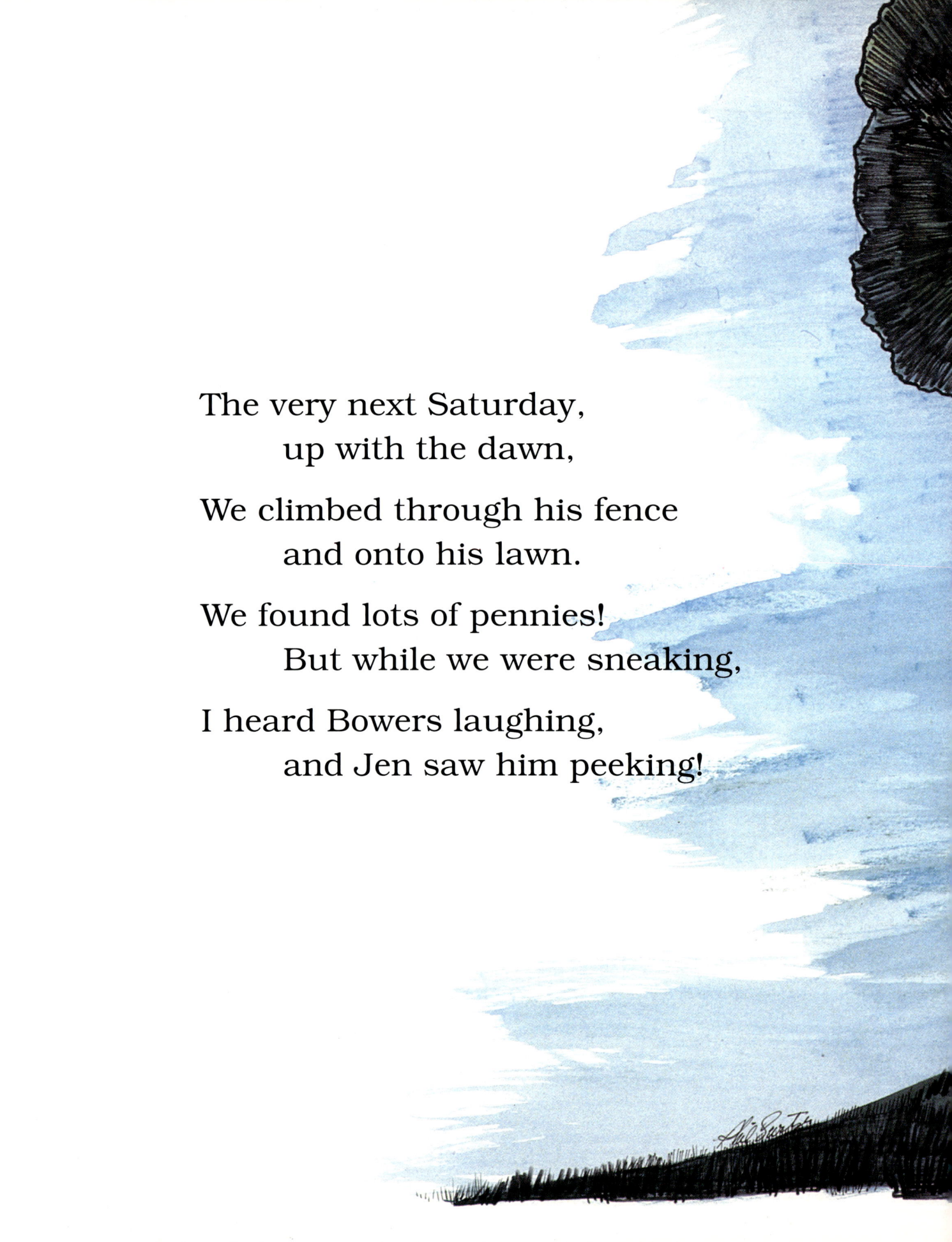

The very next Saturday,
    up with the dawn,

We climbed through his fence
    and onto his lawn.

We found lots of pennies!
    But while we were sneaking,

I heard Bowers laughing,
    and Jen saw him peeking!

For weeks, it was
    just like a magical spell.

The tree stayed green
    and pennies still fell.

We learned Mr. Bowers
    wasn't so mean.

He was the nicest guy
    we'd ever seen!

He asked us in
for "coffee breaks,"

With lots of milk
and homemade cakes.

He talked about pirates,
old friends, and old times;

He taught us his songs,
his jokes, and his rhymes.

He told of the days
    when he was a lad,

How he had dreamed then
    of the map we now had.

We'd sit on his porch
    and talk for hours,

Just Jen, and me,
    and our friend Mr. Bowers.

We couldn't wait
     for the week to end.

We'd go over early
     to visit our friend.

But then in October
as dead leaves fell,

Mr. Bowers went away,
he wasn't so well.

We searched and searched but never found,

Another penny on the ground.

I guess without our friend Mr. Bowers,

The Penny Tree had lost its powers.

Sure, we missed the coins we used to spend,

But most of all we missed our friend.

The years passed by, Jen moved away.

We said goodbye on that sad day.

I still miss Jen, now I'm old and grey,

But I still look forward to Saturday,

When lots of children visit me —

For in my back yard there's a nickel tree!

Will Reese (right) is a storyteller, author, actor, inventor, playwright and teacher. In addition to his books, he has written both fiction and nonfiction for children and adults in magazines and newspapers. He also writes and performs in radio and television programs.

Dr. Reese taught science education at the University of Alberta for thirty years. He is a life member and former president of the Alberta branch of the Canadian Authors Association. His programs of *Original Stories and Science Magic* have delighted children and adults in schools, libraries, concert halls and on many passenger ships. His most recent book, *Edmond and the Talent Stone*, was an award winner and a Best of the Best selection.

Will lives in Edmonton with his actress wife, Barbara. He is especially proud of their children and the eight grandchildren who sometimes inspire his stories.

Phil Switzer (left) finds he has more time to devote to his own painting and sculpture since his retirement. He is an active member of the potters guild in St. Albert, Alberta, and is currently working on a ceramic mural for St. Albert. During his career he was involved with theatre set design, painting and television graphics. He and Willard Reese first met in the sixties when they worked together on Alberta School Telecasts, the first of several projects to benefit from their combined efforts.